D1281474

Mr. Tanner

written by Harry Chapin
illustrated by Bryan Langdo

Ripple Grove
Press

This book is dedicated to Martin Tubridy, the real Mr. Tanner. Harry read a review of Martin's Town Hall debut in *The New York Times* and was inspired to write his song, "Mr. Tanner," which in turn led to the idea for this book. —Sandra Chapin

For my son, Oliver. —Bryan Langdo

A portion of the proceeds from the sale of this book will help support WhyHunger.

WhyHunger is a global non-profit founded in 1975 by the late musician and activist Harry Chapin and radio DJ Bill Ayres. Inspired by Harry's vision of a world free from hunger and with social justice for all, WhyHunger is building the movement to end hunger and poverty by connecting people to nutritious, affordable food and by supporting grassroots solutions that inspire self-reliance and community empowerment. WhyHunger works to support, resource, and build the capacity of community organizations and social movements that are changing the systems, policies, and institutions that perpetuate hunger and poverty in our world. They are transforming the collective food system into one that is socially and economically just, nourishes whole communities, cools the planet, and ensures the rights of all people to food, land, water, and sustainable livelihoods. Learn more at whyhunger.org.

Ripple Grove Press would like to thank Sandra Chapin and the Chapin Family for making this book possible; Pegge Strella, for helping us along the way; Howard Fields and "Big" John Wallace, for sharing their Harry and "Mr. Tanner" stories; and Bryan Langdo, for illustrating this beautiful book.

First Edition 2017
Library of Congress Control Number 2016957313
ISBN 978-0-9913866-8-0

10 9 8 7 6 5 4 3 2 1
Printed in South Korea

This book was typeset in Grit Primer.
The illustrations were rendered in watercolor.
Book design by Bryan Langdo

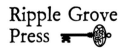

Ripple Grove
Press
Portland, OR
www.RippleGrovePress.com

MR. TANNER was a cleaner
from a town in the Midwest.

And of all the cleaning shops around
he'd made his the best.

CLEANERS

Tubridy Lane   Dayton, OH

DATE _____

NAME _____

PHONE _____

QTY	MON	TUES	WED	THU	FRI	SAT
TROUSERS						

He also was a baritone who sang while hanging clothes.

He practiced scales
while pressing tails
and sang at local shows.

His friends and neighbors praised the voice
that poured out from his throat.

They said that he should use his gift
instead of cleaning coats.

But music was his life, it was not his livelihood,

and it made him feel so happy and it made him feel so good.

He sang from his heart and he sang from his soul.

He did not know how well he sang, it just made him whole.

His friends kept working on him to try music out full time.

A big debut and rave reviews,
a great career to climb.

Finally they got to him,
he would take the fling.
A concert agent in New York
agreed to have him sing.

CIRCLE AIRLINES

MARTIN TANNER

flight: 1973

gate: H5

seat: 012

DAYTON, OH
to
NEW YORK, NY

There were plane tickets, phone calls,
money spent to rent the hall.
It took most of his savings
but he gladly used them all.

But music was his life, it was not his livelihood,
and it made him feel so happy and it made him feel so good.
He sang from his heart and he sang from his soul.
He did not know how well he sang, it just made him whole.

The evening came, he took the stage, his face set in a smile.

In the half-filled hall the critics sat watching on the aisle.

The concert was a blur to him,
spatters of applause.

He did not know how well he sang,
he only heard the flaws.

But the critics were concise, it only took four lines.
And no one could accuse them of being over kind.

Mr. Martin Tanner, Baritone, of Dayton, Ohio, made his Town Hall debut last night.

He came well prepared but unfortunately his presentation was not up to contemporary professional standards.

His voice lacks the range of tonal color necessary to make it consistently interesting.

Full-time consideration of another endeavor might be in order.

He came home to Dayton and was questioned by his friends.
But he smiled and just said nothing, and he never sang again.

Excepting very late at night
when the shop was dark and closed,
he sang softly to himself
as he sorted through the clothes.

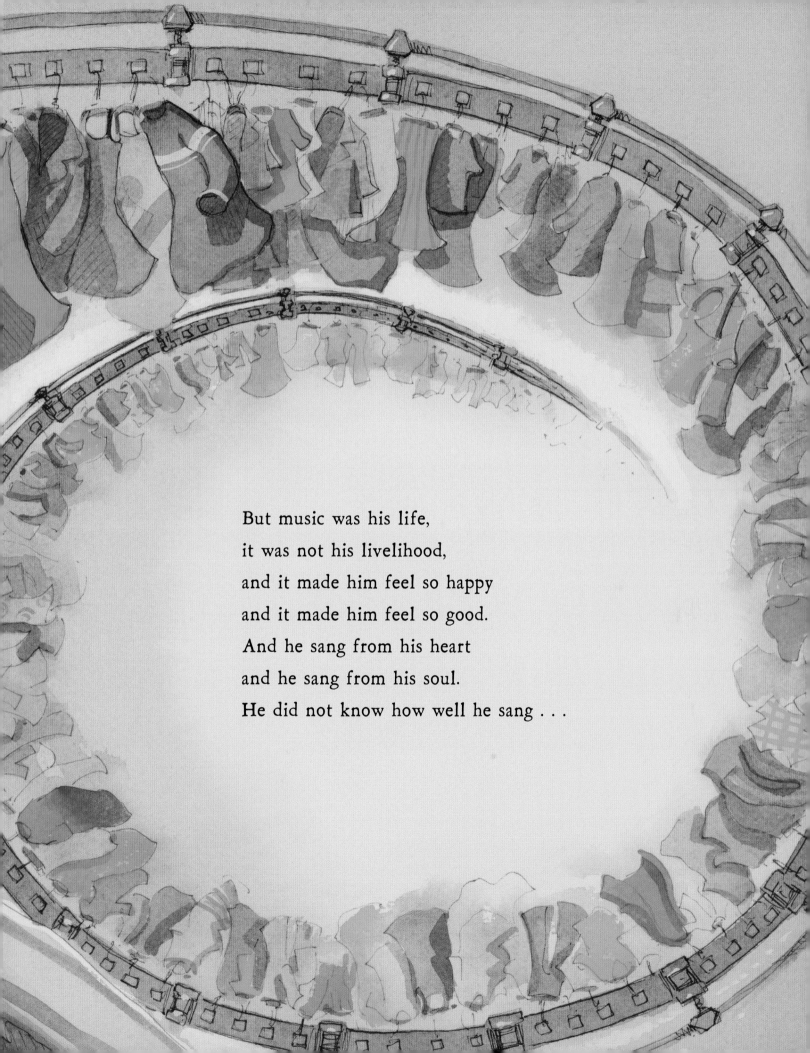

But music was his life,
it was not his livelihood,
and it made him feel so happy
and it made him feel so good.
And he sang from his heart
and he sang from his soul.
He did not know how well he sang . . .

it just made him whole.

MR. TANNER

Mr. Tanner was a cleaner from a town in the Midwest.
Of all the cleaning shops around he'd made his the best
But he also was a baritone who sang while hanging clothes
He practiced scales while pressing tales and sang at local shows
His friends and neighbors praised the voice that poured out from his throat
They told him he should use his gifts instead of cleaning coats

            But music was his life, it was not his livelyhood
            And it made him feel so happy and it made him feel so good
            He sang from his heart and he sang from his soul
            He did not know how well he sang, it just made him whole.

His friends kept working on him to try music out full time
A big debut and rave reviews, a great career to climb
Finally they got to him, he would take the fling
A concert agent in New York agreed to have him sing
There were plane tickets, phone calls, money spent to rent the hall
It took most of his savings but he'd gladly spent them all

The evening came, he took the stage, his face set in a smile
In the half-filled hall the critics sat watching on the aisle
The concert was a blur to him, spatters of applause
He did not know how well he'd done, he only heard the flaws
The critics were concise, they only took four lines
And no one could accuse them of being over kind.

            Mr. Martin Tanner of Dayton Ohio made his town hall debut last night.
            He came well prepared but unfortunately his presentation was not up to
            Contemporary professional standards. Full time consideration of
            another endevor might be in order. His voice lacks the range & tonal
            color necessary to make it consistently interesting.

He came home to Dayton and was questioned by his friends
But he smiled and just said nothing but he never sang again
Excepting very late at night when the shop was dark and closed
He sang softly to himself as he sorted through the clothes.